IMAGINE

THE TEN PLAGUES

IMAGINE

THE TEN PLAGUES

Matt
Koceich

BARBOUR BOOKS

An Imprint of Barbour Publishing, Inc.

Cover illustration: Simon Mendez

Published by Barbour Books, an imprint of Barbour Publishing, Inc., 1810 Barbour Drive, Uhrichsville, Ohio 44683, www.barbourbooks.com

Our mission is to inspire the world with the life-changing message of the Bible.

Member of the
Evangelical Christian
Publishers Association

THOUSANDS OF YEARS AGO

The horse galloped hard and carried the girl toward freedom. A hundred yards away, two massive walls of water had been pulled back to expose a narrow stretch of dry land. The girl, using her last ounce of strength, kicked her legs, trying to spur the horse on. All she had to do was reach the other side.

A second horse behind her, mounted by an Egyptian guard, closed the gap. The chase was almost over.

Even though the young girl had put up an honorable fight, the pharaoh's warrior was seconds away from catching his human prey. He rode up beside her and grabbed the back of her shirt.

Only a short time before, eleven-year-old Kai Wells had been standing at the edge of the Pi-Hahiroth camp, overlooking the sea. After an intense battle with the skilled soldier who wanted her dead, Kai couldn't fight anymore. She managed to land a last kick that connected with the warrior's knee, which allowed her to jump on the horse and ride away.

But none of that mattered now. Her heroic fight and escape were for nothing.

Her captor squeezed hard and yanked her from the fleeing horse.

The guard threw her body down, into the water.

The force was so strong it felt like she hit dry ground.

Ahead, on the freedom path, her eyes focused on the thousands of men and women and their children who were marching on, celebrating their epic escape from captivity. They had no idea what was happening to the young girl who tried so desperately to protect one of their own.

The impact of hitting the water stunned Kai. She lost her bearings. Her body was numb. The warrior had dismounted and was standing over her. Pure evil emanated from his eyes.

The end was here. The only thing Kai could think about was the little Hebrew girl she had fought so hard to protect. At least she was free. Never to be bullied by the wicked man standing over her.

The soldier who had been pursuing her since Goshen reached down and yanked Kai to her feet. The man's free hand moved to slap Kai's face. She managed to reach out and block the shot with one hand. Anger tightened the man's grip.

Kai wondered what this man was going to do to her. Three more soldiers on horseback appeared. They formed a loose circle around Kai and the soldier. Kai's guess was they had come to give help to her captor. All she wanted to do was be back home, safe in her living room, tucked under her favorite blanket staring at the fish swimming back and forth in the tank. She wondered if the fish knew there was more to the world than just the fake seaweed and sand. Kai wondered if the fish ever thought about getting out. Escaping the walls that held them in.

Ahead, a sea of people continued on, moving toward a new reality. A reality that included making their own decisions and experiencing the satisfaction that would come with that freedom. In all their celebrating, Kai's call for help was drowned out. She was past the point of being saved.

"You were a fool to think you'd escape!"

The words that came from the soldier's mouth were truth now. They took on form and entered her mind like a dagger. Kai felt them penetrate her spirit and release the last drops of willpower she'd been holding on to.

She looked out one last time at the Israelites and saw them vanish as the massive walls of water slammed shut over the narrow path of dry ground. The sea quickly wrapped up Kai and carried her away.

The fight was finished.

And so was Kai.

CHAPTER 1

PRESENT DAY

FLORIDA

Kai Wells clenched her fists and stared hard at the girl who stood across from her. Her friends had left her alone, each scampering off to safe places, far away from the towering threat known as Vivian Gold. It had come to this: a face-to-face confrontation, off school property so no teachers would ruin the fight.

Kai kept her eyes locked on the tall girl with tangled black hair who faced her. *The bully.*

Vivian Gold. The human monster that quiet people feared. *Anger. Threats. Pain.* Kai tried a quick assessment of possible escape routes, but there weren't any. Not today.

"I'm going to teach you a lesson on how to keep your pretty little mouth shut, *Wells*." The bully said Kai's last name like it was a bad word.

A young man jogged toward them, white earbuds in, oblivious to Kai's predicament. He even smiled and waved at her as he ran by.

"Vivian, this is ridiculous. We used to be friends. Played soccer at recess together. Why are you doing this?"

But Kai already knew the answer. She was just buying time. A month ago, she went to the bathroom after recess and saw Vivian shove another girl into one of the stalls. The girl asked her to stop, but Vivian had a much different agenda, and stopping wasn't on it. Her idea of justice was a hard shove and a handful of punches. Vivian yelled at the girl. . .something about not bringing extra lunch money. Kai tried standing between the two girls, but Vivian shoved her out of the way. That's when their teacher walked in and saw Kai on the ground with Vivian looming over her.

"You just had to play hero and get in my way. Mr. Kay called my mother, and I got grounded. She took away my party too. All because you had to stick your nose where it didn't belong."

Vivian closed the gap between herself and Kai. She smiled. Her loose-fitting red shirt was the color of blood and hung all the way down to her knees. Her jeans were smeared with grass stains.

Kai ignored the girl's rude words. It was one thing to have a bad day and say something unkind, but Vivian Gold was every bad day wrapped into an oversized body who spoke fluent Mean. Kai considered her options, but there weren't any. It was time to face her fears.

She unclenched her fists. "You shouldn't have hurt that girl. Doing that because she didn't give you her money was dumb."

Vivian shoved Kai. "And you should mind your own business. It's your fault this is happening."

Kai regained her balance. Even if she lost the fight, she wasn't going to turn her back on this girl. She took a deep breath. Her phone was in her backpack. She'd call her father to come pick her up.

Two new girls came running up from the school parking lot. Kai quickly saw who they were and that they weren't coming to help.

"Hey girls," Vivian said. "Just in time to watch me knock out Wells. It's going to be epic."

Kai reached around for her backpack. As she knelt

down to unzip it, Vivian's right hand shot forward and snatched it away. "Good try, punk."

Vivian reached into the backpack. She fished around and came out holding Kai's cell phone. "This what you were looking for?"

"Give me that." Kai knew the order was useless on Vivian but tried anyway.

"Ha! I'm going to give you one last chance to avoid a miserable ending to this day. One chance."

"One last chance to do what?"

Vivian looked confused. "Really?"

Kai shrugged her shoulders. "I have no idea what you're talking about."

"I'm giving you the chance to forget everything you saw in the bathroom. I'm giving you the chance to tell Mr. Kay that you were mistaken and that I wasn't doing anything to that 'poor girl.'"

Kai lunged forward in hopes of grabbing her phone, but Vivian was too tall. She raised the phone just out of Kai's reach.

"Kai, I used to think you were really cool. I even remember my first day of school. I was the new kid, and you made me feel welcome."

Kai remembered. Vivian had on the same oversized red shirt and the same dirty jeans. All the other kids were afraid to approach her, but Kai went up to her anyway. "Then why are you doing this?"

Vivian walked Kai's phone over to the gutter where a storm drain waited like a hungry, openmouthed creature eager to be fed. "I'm done talking. If you want this back, you will listen carefully and do what I say."

The two girls, Vivian's toadies, came up and stood right behind Kai.

"Go ahead." Kai was ready to get her phone back and go home.

More kids were walking toward her, interested now in watching the scene unfold.

"I'm going to give you some responsibilities, and if you do your best with them, then you'll enjoy the rest of your school year."

Kai closed her eyes and wondered what on earth Vivian Gold was about to propose. Whatever it was, Kai wanted no part of the plan. All she wanted was her phone back.

"First, you're going to school tomorrow and you will tell Mr. Kay that I had nothing to do with that girl *falling* in the bathroom. Got it?"

Kai was not about to lie for this bully. But she wanted her phone back. "Got it."

Vivian tossed Kai's cell phone down the storm drain.

"What are you doing? I just said I'd do what you asked!"

Vivian inched closer. "*Please*. I'm not stupid. We both know you said that just to get your phone back."

The girls behind Kai shoved her forward. Now she was a foot away from Vivian Gold's bloodred shirt.

"But now that I have your attention, I think you might start meaning what you say."

Somehow more kids materialized, standing in a sloppy circle around Kai and her nemesis. One kid started talking louder than the others. The word *fight* rose above the rumbling of expectant voices.

"Vivian—"

Just as the name came out, the girl in the bloodred shirt shoved Kai with more power than the first time.

The sound of *fight* got louder and louder. Kai didn't

want to fight, but she didn't want to run away.

The bully closed the space between them, palms open.

"Vivian, you're making a mistake. You're going to—"

"Shut your mouth!" Vivian Gold's right fist exploded outward, connecting with Kai's face. Her world flashed white from the pain.

Yelling and cheering rang through Kai's brain, mixing with the hurt and confusion. She thought she saw a teacher running up to stop the fight. Kai tried to shake off the blow, but she stumbled backward. This time, the girls behind her moved out of the way and let her fall.

Kai felt someone catch her. She was still trying to get her bearings, but she was certain it was a teacher. All she could make out were long blue sleeves that covered the person's arms. Pain shot through her, causing Kai to keep her eyes closed.

More shouts. This time from the one who caught her.

"Everyone, go home!"

Kai thought she heard a second command. It sounded like, *"Open her eyes,"* but that didn't make sense. Kai was just confused because of being hit and then falling.

Kai pushed back against the pain and opened her eyes, but what she saw wasn't what she expected.

What she saw blew her mind.

CHAPTER 2

ANCIENT EGYPT

An unseen power seemed to erase the neighborhood from around Kai. The street, Vivian, and the collection of onlookers were wiped away in the blink of an eye.

Literally.

But in the wake of her world disappearing, a flood of new sights that made a completely new land came like the soft, comforting tendrils of a wonderful dream.

The sidewalk Kai had been standing on was now a field of tall, swaying grass. Next to the field ran a wide indigo river. A radiant sun cast its rays over the water making the surface sparkle like it was covered in diamonds. Kai blinked, expecting Vivian's harsh face to be back in front of her. But the idyllic scene remained.

As mesmerizing as it was, Kai began to panic. She reached for her cell phone. Calling her dad would solve this problem. He'd get in the car and come pick her up. He'd reassure her everything was going to be okay. He'd tell some jokes on the ride home, and the stress of Vivian Gold would be washed away. But then Kai remembered her phone was now lying at the bottom of the sewer. And her mom was out of town on another business trip, so she was out of options.

Kai's imagination ran ahead of her, making her start to believe that she had somehow been transported to a faraway place. A magical land where sunlit, diamond rivers made their way through fields of deepest green.

Kai laughed. This whole change in scenery was nothing more than her brain's version of "seeing stars" after being beat down by Vivian Gold. She turned around, trying to test her theory. But where the school should have been, there was now a wide-open field with three grazing horses, all the color of midnight.

Kai started walking toward the beautiful creatures. As she got closer, they stopped eating and raised their heads to consider if she was a threat. After a few seconds, they lowered their heads and resumed their grazing. With a few more courageous steps, Kai reached the closest of the three horses. She put out her hand to touch it, when she heard a shout.

"Don't touch them!" A man's voice ordered her to stop.

Kai froze at the sound. It had just been her and the horses in the field. Now she turned and saw a young man. He wore a sand-colored tunic that came down to his knees and nothing on his feet. His black hair was cropped short and stopped above his ears. As he stepped closer, Kai noticed he wore black eyeliner.

"Those horses belong to the pharaoh."

The pharaoh?

Where in the world am I?

There was something about the man's deep voice that made Kai feel she wasn't in danger. She stuck out a hand to greet him. "I'm Kai."

The stranger stared at her for a while. "Kai?"

"Yes. What's your name?"

The man put his hand out and shook Kai's. "My name is Amenken, but everyone calls me Amen."

Kai smiled. "Amen, like the end of a prayer. Cool."

The man looked at Kai like she was out of her mind.

"What do you mean?"

"A-m-e-n, amen. Like, *God, please help me. . . Amen.*"

"No, not *ay. Ah* like Ah-min. Like, *Hello, my name is Amenken.*"

Kai laughed, and the man did too. She turned to look at the horses again.

"Amen, I mean Ah-min. . ."

"Yes, Kai." The man stood next to her and faced the animals.

"You said the horses belong to the pharaoh?"

"Yes, Kai. Ramesses."

Kai felt light-headed. She blinked a few times. Vivian had obviously hit her so hard she was seeing a handsome man wearing black eyeliner and beautiful horses grazing in a field. "Where am I?"

"Kai, you are here in Pi-Ramesses. That river over there is a branch of the mighty Nile. Now, may I ask you a question?"

As much as Kai would rather be in this beautiful place instead of back home fighting with Vivian Gold, something wasn't right. "What—what am I doing here?"

"Kai. . ." Amenken regarded the horses for a while. "Kai, I don't know the answer to that question."

"Okay, what was your question?"

"Where are you from? I've never seen anyone dressed like you are."

"I'm from Florida. Do you know where that is?"

Amenken paused and thought about Kai's answer. "No, I've never heard of this Florida. Is it as beautiful as our home?"

Kai laughed. "Yes." Then after a pause she asked, "Can you show me around?"

Amenken led Kai up a dirt path that cut through the field, leaving the horses behind. The path quickly gave way to a dirt road that led all the way to the edge of the Egyptian city. At the crest of the hill that marked the end of Pi-Ramesses, the land fell back down into a wide-open valley. Filled with makeshift shelters, the valley was like a human sea.

"The Israelites."

"You mean like Moses?" Kai couldn't take her eyes off the crowd of people that filled the valley.

"Do you know him too?"

"Yes. I mean no, not really. I've read about him hundreds of times."

Amenken pointed to a cluster of tiny tent shelters closest to where they were standing. "That's where the one named Moses stays. The pharaoh's guards move on horseback all day and night around the perimeter of the valley making sure the people down there don't try to escape."

Kai couldn't believe it! She was actually experiencing the epic Bible story where Moses had to confront the pharaoh and help lead the Israelites to freedom. Past the soldiers on horseback. Through the Red Sea. And all of that only after the ten plagues fell over the land. Crazy enough to imagine, let alone be a part of it. "Earlier you said you needed my help?"

Amenken continued, "Yes. There's a young Hebrew girl named Lily. She was caught bringing water from the Nile to her family. One of the guards threatened the girl's father, saying he would hurt Lily's mother if the girl continued to take water from the sacred river."

Kai already felt a connection to Lily. The guard was acting like a bully if he had a problem with a little girl getting water for her family.

Amenken grabbed Kai by the arm. "Come, we have to hurry. The guards are approaching." He started back in the direction of the city. Kai kept pace.

"All the Hebrew people are here to work for Ramesses. They are given a meager amount of food and water each day. I asked Lily why she also goes to get more water from the river. She told me her family gives it to the sick. That the portion they get during the day isn't enough."

Kai looked over at Amenken. "Why are we running?"

"I work for the pharaoh's guard. I make the blades they wield in battle. I am at the river more than anyone to cool off from all the fire used in my work. I met Lily, and my heart was moved by her story." The man stopped talking and looked over his shoulder. He picked up the pace. Kai somehow managed to keep up.

"I started helping Lily get the water back to her people. One of the guards, Horus, saw me come from the valley. His name means 'falcon.' He knows something is going on. He constantly watches."

The pair jogged farther down the dirt path in silence. Kai couldn't help thinking her dream was so realistic.

Just minutes ago she was being shoved around by Vivian Gold, and now she was running across an ancient Egyptian city.

"STOP!" The booming voice came from one in authority.

Kai didn't have to turn around to see who issued the command.

The bird of prey.

The falcon.

CHAPTER 3

Kai followed her new friend through a maze of houses and backstreets. Past men and women who looked at her as though an alien spaceship had just dropped her off. Kai looked back and was grateful to see the guard was no longer in pursuit.

Winded, she was relieved when Amenken finally stopped in front of a house with a spacious courtyard in front.

"Hurry inside. This is our home."

A woman appeared in the doorway.

"My wife, Betrest."

Kai shook the woman's hand. Amenken moved behind the older lady. "Come, beloved. Horus has followed us from the fields, and it was not to shake our hands."

"Should I make a meal for our guest?" Betrest asked.

"Yes, and I will stay outside in case the falcon returns."

Amenken's wife invited Kai to help prepare a simple meal that resembled a fish soup with flatbread. There were three small bowls filled with dates, peas, and beans.

"We are glad you are here. The others who have come before were like family to me and my husband."

"Others?"

"Yes, people who dress as you. You are not the first to visit."

Kai had no idea how any of this was happening. She couldn't understand how she was able to experience. . . This place. This time. She shook her head in disbelief.

The sun soon disappeared, replaced by a darkness Kai had not felt back home. Here in this otherworld, the night came like an army of silent shadows.

Amenken returned, worry lines etched across his face. "Horus sent one of his men with threats. If I help you, there will be consequences."

Kai's brain was on overload. For some reason, here in this place, she was a threat. That was hilarious. "I don't want to be a problem. I just don't understand how I got here."

Amenken smiled, losing his worried look. "We'll take care of you. Everything will work out at the right time. It always does."

Betrest placed three wicker mats on the ground in a triangle. "Sit."

Kai obeyed. This was a far cry from her family's dining room table, but there was something intimate about sharing a meal like this. Amenken sat on another mat, while Betrest placed the food in the middle.

Kai had a random thought about her dad. Was he looking for her? Was he freaking out because she wasn't home from school yet? How long had it been since she arrived in this foreign land?

The food tasted surprisingly good. The three ate in silence and didn't take long to finish the meal.

"Kai, I need you to rest." Amenken grabbed his soup bowl and stood. "Even though we don't know what tomorrow holds, I do know that Horus will do his best to keep things interesting."

The man walked over and put the bowl down next to a big ceramic pitcher. He grabbed a rolled-up rug and turned to Kai. "You will sleep in our room with Betrest. I am going to stay outside on watch. Just in case."

Just in case?

Kai got up and followed Amenken into a small room that was connected to the kitchen area. He unrolled the rug on the floor and straightened it out for his guest. This was crazy. No bed. No pillow.

Kai got down on the rug and lay on her side, using her hands to prop her head. As primitive as it was, she felt safe. And for all the insanity that had happened that day—from Vivian Gold to being chased through the streets of an ancient Egyptian city by a pharaoh's guard—it felt good to rest.

ooooo

Kai woke to an unfamiliar room illuminated by rays of sunlight. She found Amen's wife near the fire holding a large loaf of bread, much bigger than the one they had shared for dinner. Kai looked out the window and saw Amen outside in the courtyard holding a small silver dagger.

"Good morning, Kai. I hope you slept well."

"Morning, Betrest." Kai smiled. "I did get sleep. Thank you."

But Kai wanted to be back home in Florida, even if it meant dealing with the Vivian Golds of the world. She didn't belong here.

When Kai stepped out into the new morning, Amen put the tiny blade on the ground and greeted her with a fatherly embrace. Kai looked over his shoulder and saw the blade had a cool red gemstone inlaid just above the handle.

"Follow me."

Amen led her to the same field from yesterday, where the horses grazed and the beautiful blue river flowed. Palm trees of all sizes stood side by side along the banks, their peaceful fronds swaying in the steady breeze, and towering sand dunes reached up to touch the sky. This time there were no horses, but instead, three men stood side by side at the water's edge. The sun was just above the horizon, painting the new day in streaks of orange and red.

"Kai, these men are the Hebrew brothers, Moses and Aaron. And the one on the right is the pharaoh."

Moses?

Aaron?

The pharaoh?

"Is the man holding the staff Moses?"

"Yes," Amen replied. "Yesterday, the brother Aaron threw the staff down in front of Pharaoh, and it became a snake!"

Kai remembered some of the details. "The pharaoh's men made their staffs turn into serpents also, but then Aaron's staff swallowed up all the others."

Amenken's mouth dropped open. "How did you know that?"

Kai told the man about the Bible, but he just shook his head like he was the one having a crazy experience in some faraway place where young kids knew things they had no business knowing.

Amen led Kai closer to the water. She could hear the conversation clearly now.

"Let them go so we may worship God in the desert."

Moses hadn't finished his sentence before Pharaoh shook his head in a dismissive gesture.

"Pharaoh, let us go and worship. Let my people go. If you don't, your river and all your water will be turned into blood."

Kai watched in disbelief as the royal man disregarded

the threat Moses gave.

Then, Aaron raised the staff out over the Nile River and struck the water. Immediately, dark bands of water swirled in scarlet spirals out from the place where the staff had touched the surface.

The pharaoh watched as the water became a river of blood. He shook his head a second time and walked away.

Kai stared at the river of blood. Dead fish were starting to rise to the surface. "Amen, this is really happening! I can't believe this is really happening!"

Amenken took Kai's hands, attempting to calm her down despite the fact the Nile River had just turned into blood. "What is all this? You have knowledge of something greater than I. Tell me, child. Tell me."

Suddenly distant screams came from the village.

Moses and Aaron turned and started walking toward Kai and Amenken.

Kai couldn't remove her gaze from the blood river. *Insane!*

"Amen, the Bible says that this blood in the water is the first of ten plagues."

"Ten?"

Kai nodded. "And they only get worse!"

Amen grabbed Kai's hand. "Come. We need to hurry."

Amenken led Kai back to his house. More screams could be heard coming from nearby homes. Betrest stood in the courtyard holding an earthen jar. Her eyes were filled with terror.

"What is it?" Amenken asked.

"Blood! Our water has turned to blood!"

Amenken took the clay jar and set it down. "Please, Betrest, do not fear. I will go to Lily and her family. They will help us."

ooooo

Screams filled the air like a sick chorus of voices signaling the end of the world.

Amenken led Kai back through the village. "We are going to the valley where the Israelites are camped. You probably know about the Israelites too?"

Kai nodded.

Their path took them past three lakes. All three bodies of water had turned to blood. The air smelled putrid—like rotten meat.

"What did you say was wrong with the girl getting water from the Nile?"

Amenken looked at Kai like she might possibly be sick. "Like I was saying, only Egyptians take water from the sacred river. The Hebrews are not allowed to. Pharaoh's men deliver water to camp once a day to be rationed. It's unfortunate, because many die from dehydration."

"What happened with Lily?"

"When I stopped her, she said her mother was sick. She said she was taking the clean water back to help her feel better. As I mentioned, I started helping her so she wouldn't get caught."

Kai stopped and glanced back at the city. All the Egyptian villagers were scurrying around with their clay pots. Dark liquid sloshed out where water should have been. She watched as the people ran in the direction of the Nile. When they reached the wide river, they dropped to their knees and started clawing at the ground. Kai recalled the Exodus account. *And all the Egyptians dug along the Nile to get drinking water, because they could not drink the water of the river."*

Amenken led Kai down a winding dirt path into the valley. The sight was unbelievable. The entire valley was dotted with cream-colored makeshift tents. Thousands and thousands of tents. . .

As they got closer to the camp, Kai saw a group of children chasing each other around a large tent. There was one young girl who played by herself, throwing stones at a withered tree. Kai saw she had tan skin and matted brown hair that tried to hang in loose curls, and she wore a dirty fabric dress that had probably been white a long time ago.

"That's Lily," Amenken said.

Kai thought the little girl could pass for a younger version of herself.

"She looks like she's your sister."

"I know, Amen. I just thought the same thing!"

"There she is!" Amenken's voice broke through Kai's thoughts on all that she was experiencing. "Hurry. I need to get to her before Horus and the guards come back."

The girl saw Amenken and waved. She quickly disappeared into the closest tent.

Kai and Amenken followed. When they peered inside, Kai saw the little girl was the only one home. She was standing in front of a curtain, arms at her sides.

Amenken stepped inside. Again, Kai followed.

"Horus!"

A man's voice sounded from somewhere nearby. Amenken looked at Kai.

"It's one of the guards. He's calling Horus by name. Must be a close acquaintance." Amenken put his right index finger to his lips. Lily copied the gesture, moving her own finger to her lips. Amenken nodded his approval.

"Horus! They have clean water! We've found where the girl has been storing it." The guard's voice was closer now. Just outside the tent.

Kai put her hands on Lily's shoulders. It felt like the right thing to do.

"Horus?"

The guard's shadow stretched across the tent opening. Mere feet separated them from being discovered. Seconds passed that seemed like an eternity. Lily never budged.

"I'm in here." The official who had chased them only yesterday now stepped out from behind the curtain. "I'm in here with Amenken, the traitor."

The falcon had them cornered.

This time his prey would not escape.

CHAPTER 4

"Dear Amenken." The falcon shook his head like he was the parent scolding a child. "You disappoint me. You are a disgrace and should be ashamed of yourself."

Amenken turned to Kai. "Take the girl outside so we can talk."

"Not so fast." Pharaoh's official grabbed Lily and pulled her to his side. "She stays with me."

Kai's thoughts flashed back to the sidewalk in Florida. The way the man named Horus touched the little girl was the same way Vivian Gold pushed people around. Kai didn't know how the rules worked here in this ancient place, but she was overwhelmed with the feeling that she had to protect Lily.

"Let the child go," Amenken said. "I am the one you're after."

"Oh, how noble of you." Horus kept his right hand on Lily's shoulder. Kai stared at the man's odd outfit. He wore only a short linen skirt tied at the waist and brown leather sandals. "I have a rather ironic idea. I should tell Pharaoh that I will use the next sword you forge to teach you a lesson."

Amenken didn't flinch. Kai saw his eyes move from Lily to the tent opening. Kai couldn't overpower Horus. She had no clue how she could get the young girl out of this mess.

At the exact same moment, the tent flap opened and a man wearing a similar outfit to what Horus was wearing appeared. The only difference was that this guy had a broad leather band wrapped around his torso. He was holding a clay jar. "Sir, just making sure you're okay."

"I'm fine. More blood there?" Horus pointed at the man's jar.

The newcomer bent down and stepped into the tent. "Sir, this is truly unbelievable. See for yourself." He offered the clay jar to his comrade.

Horus took it and stuck a finger in and pulled it back out.

"Water."

"Yes, sir. All of *their* jars contain water." The man pointed at Lily as he spoke.

Horus turned Lily to face him. "By what magic do you do this? Tell me!"

Kai's brain wasn't working as fast as she'd like. She had to get the girl away from this man. "I know how." The words were out even though Kai didn't know what was coming next. They served a purpose because now she had both officials' full attention.

Horus considered Kai. "Who are you, anyway? By what you cover yourself in, I'd say you are from very far away."

Real far. "My name is Kai. Rhymes with sky. I'm from a place called Florida. Our customs are very different than yours. I cover myself in jeans and a white shirt." Kai glanced at Lily then noticed sunlight flickering through a slit in the back of the tent. The fabric was loose where it met the ground.

Loose enough for a little girl to slip out of. . .

"Tell me about the water." The falcon was getting irritated. He clenched his fists like they were talons grabbing for a thick tree branch.

Amenken hadn't moved. Kai wished she could communicate her plan with him, but she had no plan. All she wanted was for Lily to be able to run out the opening in the back of the tent. That's when she recalled how Vivian Gold snatched her backpack. Kai remembered looking for her phone when the bully attacked. . . .

It was worth a shot. She had to make a move that would cause Horus to flinch.

Kai let out a scream and jumped toward the newcomer. Horus let go of Lily to stop Kai. The newcomer let go of the jar to put his hands up to keep Kai away.

The plan worked and Lily slipped away and out the back of the tent.

The jar broke into three large shards.

The newcomer grabbed Kai.

Kai dropped to her knees and grabbed one of the shards.

The falcon swooped in.

Kai ran the shard into the newcomer's arm. He let her go for a split second.

Horus lunged at Kai and would have captured her,

but Amenken jumped in front of the man to block his attack.

Kai used the few seconds of freedom to rush out the front of the tent. Once outside, she snaked her way through hundreds of tents. Eventually, she caught up with the Hebrew girl.

They continued to race through the massive tent city until it was clear their hunter had given up the chase.

ooooo

Seven suns had risen in the sky above the camp before all the blood had washed away from the river, lakes, and canals.

Kai had managed to keep Lily safe from Horus and his henchmen by hiding out in various tents throughout the valley. Along the way, she had traded her clothes for a tunic that matched the young girl's, just different in size. More than one Hebrew family told Kai that she looked like Lily's older sister.

Kai tried returning to Amenken's home, but Horus had a guard posted there. She wanted to thank Amen for helping her and Lily escape. She wanted to tell him and his sweet Betrest that she was safe. But all of that would have to wait for another day.

Lily had taken Kai all across the Israelite camp—and a hundred days wouldn't be enough to cover the whole site, let alone seven. But in the past week since they escaped the falcon's claws, Kai had met many people who were not unlike herself. Although they were doing jobs that Kai had never done, they were all focused on a specific task like Kai was focused on helping Lily stay safe. There were women who worked in fields—strong women who wielded primitive blades and chopped wheat stalks for hours on end. Others hauled the harvested grain back to the city where the Hebrew men would use it to make brick.

Kai didn't want to draw attention to herself and knew that changing her appearance would help her stay safe from the Egyptian official. She found a Hebrew woman holding a sickle. "Can you cut my hair?"

"Daughter, your hair is beautiful. It would be a sin to cut it."

Kai explained the story and her reason for wanting to cut it off. The Hebrew woman shook her head. "Come here." After a few strokes of the blade, Kai's hair had been transformed from long, loose curls to a short, choppy, uneven mess.

After the primitive haircut, Kai made her way up into the hills where she had discovered a good hiding place. From the shelter of a boulder pile, overlooking Pi-Ramesses, Kai was able to watch the guard that had been posted in front of Amenken's house. When Amenken would leave, Kai noticed the guard would follow him.

Kai decided that she would have to contact Betrest while the guard was away.

As she made her way through the streets, Kai remained vigilant. She half expected the falcon to swoop down on her from above. Just before Kai reached Amen's house, she looked across the lake and saw two men talking to Pharaoh. One of the men held a staff, so she assumed that was Aaron. Which meant the other man was most likely Moses. The three were standing at the edge of a lake that was at the southern edge of the royal palace. Kai watched Aaron take his staff and touch the lake water.

From where she stood, it looked to Kai as though small black blobs started coming up out of the lake. The blobs were hopping. Hopping up out of the water and all over the ground surrounding the water.

Frogs!

Kai saw the creatures were now pouring from the palace windows as well. Past the city, she saw the frogs were also coming up out of the Nile. Soon, the raised voices announcing the invasion of the unwanted creatures mixed with croaking, to produce an otherworldly cacophony of sound.

Kai made her way through the commotion that had descended on the Egyptian village. As she tried to get to Amenken's house, Kai found it difficult to move quickly because of the frogs. They were jumping up at her. Big, nasty-looking ones and tiny colorful ones that resembled the poisonous frogs Kai had studied for a science project.

With every step she took, frogs were getting trapped under her feet. Where were they coming from? This was the second plague, so somehow God was making these crazy things happen. . . .

"The frogs are in my oven!"

Kai ducked behind a simple dwelling that resembled

a one-story Native American pueblo, like the replica she'd enjoyed making for social studies class. She'd used shoe boxes and modeling clay to represent the adobe that constructed the ancient dwelling. She'd even included toothpick ladders spread out across the various levels of the structure.

Frogs were jumping out of the window and doorway. A woman appeared, using her right foot to push a pile of frogs out of the home. But for all her effort, more frogs jumped in past her.

All the homes Kai could see had the same problem. Men and women alike were trying in vain, using their hands and feet as shovels to rid their abodes of the invading amphibians.

"They are in my kneading trough!"

Just as Kai fought past the frogs—they had become so numerous and deep, it was like she was trying to wade through a river—she saw Amen's house.

And Horus. The falcon was sitting on his horse, unaffected by the frogs. Kai thought the horse would be skittish, but the rider kept the animal in control.

She had to find a way to get to Amenken. But there

was no way she could without first being seen by the official.

Kai decided to wait where she was, hidden behind the corner of a house, but the frogs kept coming. The horse that the falcon rode began to get agitated. The frogs were jumping and swarming around its legs. It reared back on its hind legs, nearly sending Horus to the ground.

Kai spotted a ladder and climbed up to the roof. From the edge of the roof, she could see Amenken's house and the sea of frogs that now filled every possible space.

Nature overthrew the falcon's power to control. The horse couldn't stand it any longer. Kai watched it rear up again and then explode down the street. Horus barely held on as the creature now had full control of him.

Kai used the twist of fate to hurry back down the ladder and trudge through the frogs to get to Amenken's house. She knocked on the door, and after a while, Amen's wife opened the door.

"Get away!"

Kai was confused. Then she realized her hair had been longer and she wore normal clothes the last time she was here. "Betrest, it's me, Kai."

"I know who you are. Get away from here. You show up and these evil things happen."

How could this be? "Betrest, I have nothing to do with the blood or the frogs. Please believe me. Is Amenken here?"

"Get away! And don't come back."

Betrest slammed the door closed.

Kai didn't have another plan, so she decided to go back to Lily and her family.

She plowed through the frogs as she made her way out of the city. As soon as Kai reached the Israelite camp, she noticed there were no frogs. She made her way to Lily's tent just as the sun set and darkness covered the land.

ooooo

The next morning, word around the camp was that Moses had been asked by Pharaoh to pray for God to remove the frogs. Apparently, a young man told Kai, Pharaoh had agreed to let the Israelites go if the frog problem could be solved.

Kai needed to connect with Amenken. She told Lily that she wouldn't be gone long and headed back to the city, always keeping an eye out for Horus.

"They're dead!"

Kai heard the same phrase uttered over and over again as people found the lifeless frogs in their houses, courtyards, and fields. The air smelled so rotten that she had difficulty breathing.

Suddenly a hand touched her back. Kai jumped, feeling dread at the thought that Horus had finally caught her. But when she turned to see the owner of the hand, Kai was relieved. It was Amenken. Her surprise quickly morphed into fear as she saw that Amen's face and arms were covered in cuts. It looked like a giant cat had swiped its claws all across the man's body. His cheeks and forehead were lined with horrible wounds.

"Follow me and hurry," he said.

"What did they do to you?" Kai felt ridiculous even asking the question. The answer was obvious.

The falcon had captured his prey.

CHAPTER 5

"What on earth happened?"

Up until now, the Bible stories about the plagues on Egypt had just been words on a page for Kai. Reading about them was nothing compared to experiencing it all for herself. Kai had a brief thought of Vivian Gold and wondered what was going on back home in Florida.

Amenken led Kai down an alley between two houses, carefully navigating the piles of frogs that people were trying to get rid of. "Horus wanted to discipline me for helping you and Lily. He didn't want to make it too bad but bad enough so I would turn you in."

Kai stopped running. Then Amen stopped.

"Kai, I'm not handing you over. If I had those intentions, I could have taken you in while you were sleeping.

as been moved to help you and Lily. You have
"

Kai stood there, looking at the man with disbelief in her eyes.

"Come on, Kai. If we don't hurry, we'll both be caught and worthless to help Lily and the others."

Something moved Kai forward. Something told her to trust Amenken. "Come on. Where are we going?"

Amenken smiled and started jogging again. "That big building over there. It's called the Temple of Set."

Kai didn't know anything about the name. "Who's that?"

Amenken kept leading Kai through the stone maze of backstreets, every once in a while looking over his shoulder to see if they were being followed. "Set is one of the people's gods. They believe he rules over the deserts and storms. The villagers think Set helps protect them when disorder and violence come."

They came out of the maze onto a wide street that ran behind the pharaoh's palace and ended at the steps of a massive temple. Stone pillars that supported a flat roof rose around the perimeter of the structure. In the middle of the temple, a thick wall rose high above the roofline and was covered with drawings of faceless men and women in different poses. Small square openings dotted the wall.

Kai made an observation. "I'd think there'd be people flocking into this temple, given the plagues that are coming over them."

Amenken either didn't have an answer or was preoccupied with getting inside. "Hurry!"

As they got closer to the temple, the ground seemed to come alive beneath Kai's feet, turning from sandy soil to the color of night.

"Hurry!" Amenken grabbed her hand and pulled her on toward the mighty temple. As they ran, the earth rose up in a pulsing blanket of black bugs. In an instant, the dust of the ground had transformed into millions of insects. But as the bugs rose, they did not bother Kai.

"Gnats! It's another plague!" Kai yelled.

As they hurried up the stone ramp that led to the temple entrance, a man ran out covered in the pests. He was trying to brush them off, only more gnats rose from the ground to fill the empty places on his body. Kai shut her eyes and let Amenken lead her the rest of the way into the coolness of the temple. Once inside, Kai let her eyes adjust to the dimness. She followed Amenken, and after a few twists and turns between the pillars and a few winding hallways, he stopped again. An older man sat in a remote corner of the temple, holding a book in his weathered hands.

"Amenken. Haven't seen you in quite a while. Who's your friend?"

"Naaji, you wise old fool. Didn't think you'd still be here."

"They can't run me off, no matter how many men they send from the pharaoh's guard."

Amenken smiled. "They don't know what to do with an old man and his old imagination."

Naaji grinned. "I help people. I never beg or bother. If someone asks me for help, I help them. The guards feel like my presence hinders the citizens who come to talk to the gods."

Kai didn't understand but was too nervous to ask.

Amenken stepped aside and pulled her over so she was standing directly in front of the old man. "This is my new friend, Kai."

The old man looked at her and smiled. "Welcome, Kai. We're glad you're here."

Kai saw that he was holding an open book in his lap. More like a handmade journal.

"Don't mean to hurry, but we're being followed. Horus and his men have a problem with us."

The one named Naaji stood. "If they are after you, then take this and be on your way." He handed Kai his book.

The pages, Kai saw, were filled with sketches of kids her age but dressed much differently. Like maybe they were from a decade ago or something. "Who are these people?"

"Well," Naaji started, "they've all been able to experience this place like you are doing now."

Kai flipped through the pages a second time. She noticed there were also names and dates written beneath each of the sketches. One of the names said *COREY MAX, 2017.* He had spikey blond hair and wore a T-shirt and a pair of cargo shorts. The next name was *MARK GRANT, 1977.* He was a boy with long hair and wore an old *Star Wars* T-shirt that resembled the *New Hope* movie poster. Her dad was a Star Wars fan and constantly talked about the movie. Kai did the math and guessed that this "kid" would now be in his forties.

"That's the year he came through the temple and allowed me to sketch him," Naaji said.

"How is this going to help us with Horus?" Kai asked as she closed the journal.

"It's not. Horus isn't the main problem. There is a great enemy out there. The one who is in the world. A great unseen force. This book will help you battle him."

Kai was now officially terrified. She remembered the stories where Jesus would refer to the devil as the one who was in the world. She tried handing the book back to the old man.

"Oh no, young lady. The book is yours now. My job is done."

Amenken interrupted. "What does that mean?"

Naaji continued, "It means your little friend Kai here is the one who is supposed to take the book. It belongs to her now. It's up to her to figure out what to do with it."

Kai dropped the book on the ground. "Come on, Amen." *This guy's nuts.*

Noises sounded from behind them back near the temple entrance. Garbled voices growing louder.

The falcon had found them!

"Come on, Kai. We have to get out of here."

Naaji picked up the book. He opened it to the last page and turned it so Kai could see it. "Look familiar?"

Kai couldn't believe what her eyes saw. It was a sketch of her. At the bottom of the picture was her name: *KAI WELLS, 2018.*

Kai couldn't believe it. Wherever she was, this place kept getting crazier and crazier. "You just said the kids who came through allowed you to draw their pictures. I just met you—"

"STOP!" The voices yelled at them from behind.

Kai grabbed the book.

"Come on, Kai, we need to go!" Amenken took off running toward the back of the temple. "There's a way out back here."

Kai looked at Naaji and saw a smile on his weathered face.

"Kai," Naaji said, "your story doesn't end here in Egypt."

Kai looked back and saw the guards running in her direction. She clutched the book tighter and nodded at Naaji. Then she took off into the shadows after Amenken.

ooooo

They stepped through a small stone archway out into the daylight. Kai blinked as her eyes readjusted to the sunlight.

"Naaji showed me that secret passage. Let's hurry back to my house and make a new plan," said Amenken.

The swarms of tiny gnats filled the air like black smoke that wouldn't drift away in the wind. As Kai followed Amenken down the side steps of the temple, she saw a large crowd of people standing in the street, covered in bugs. Their arms flailed in every direction trying to rid their bodies of the gnats.

There was no way to avoid the crowd. "Come on, Kai. These people will actually help shield us from the soldiers. When they realize we're not in the back of the temple, they'll run out here and see this mob of people." He led Kai through the middle of the great crowd.

Halfway through the bug-infested mob, a hand shot out and grabbed Kai by the arm.

"She's evil! She's the reason for the plagues! Take her to Pharaoh!"

"Amenken, help!" Kai tried pulling the stranger's hand off her arm, but she wasn't strong enough.

Another voice from the crowd rose above the others. "I saw her before. These bad things started happening as soon as she got here!"

"Amenken!" Kai got pulled deeper into the crowd and lost sight of her friend. "Amenken!"

Through the confusion of the yelling and the people crowding around her, Kai saw the guards come up and move the people out of the way. "Let go of the girl!"

Kai felt the hand that was holding her release its grip. She spun around looking for Amenken. She saw him standing just past the crowd, but she couldn't move.

The gnats swirled around the crowd, but they stayed off of Kai.

The soldiers made their way to her.

She held the book behind her back.

The first soldier to reach her looked at Kai and shook his head. He also had to fight off the gnats in order to keep eye contact with Kai. "Amazing that the bugs don't affect this one. Take her to Horus. Immediately!"

CHAPTER 6

Kai found herself sitting in a primitive cell—four walls of dirt and a wooden grate to keep the prisoner in and the free world out. She remembered the journal and looked around, but the mysterious book wasn't there. Where was Amenken?

Three large, muscular men, clothed in nothing more than white wraps, stood outside her prison cell. Kai thought it was quite funny that Horus sent three massive men to guard an eleven-year-old girl. Maybe there was another reason for the three guards, but Kai couldn't figure out what it could possibly be.

No sooner had she stopped thinking about the guard situation than Kai looked up and saw Horus approaching up a wide sandy path. He had the journal in his hands.

When he arrived at Kai's cell, the three guards separated and let their commander pass by.

"Kai, this book of names here is really a mystery to me. I thought that old fool Naaji was simply a lunatic who created stories that no one would ever read. Then I find your name in this book and begin to wonder if I've been wrong this whole time." Horus motioned for one of the guards to open Kai's cell.

She remained seated, not sure what her options were. The Egyptian official sat down on the dirt floor opposite Kai.

"There's something different about you. These plagues don't seem to affect you. Tell me about that."

Kai looked at the man and hoped he would believe her confusion. "I have no idea what's going on."

"Yes, sweet girl," Horus said, rolling his eyes. "The more truthful you are, the better this is going to be."

Kai closed her eyes in prayer. *Lord, help me stand up to this guy. He's the male version of Vivian Gold. Help me get rid of him.*

"If you don't answer me, there's going to be a major problem." The falcon was getting irritated.

"I told you the truth." Kai recounted the whole story starting with Vivian's bullying.

This time Horus remained silent as he let her explanation simmer.

"Something still doesn't make sense, but I don't have time to sit here and argue with a child. I'm going to hold on to this book, and you are going to work on cleaning my city up. This wonderful little home will be where you sleep. This will be your new life until you decide to be honest with me."

"But—"

Horus stood and brushed the dirt from his clothes.

The conversation was over.

ooooo

Time passed slowly, Kai thought, like when her mom made her use the last drops of ketchup from a squeeze bottle. The swarm of gnats that had plagued the Egyptians were now just piles of black that covered the ground, turning the sand into darkness.

One of the guards knelt down and opened the grate to Kai's cell. He remained silent but waved her out. Tired of being cramped in the tiny space, Kai was more than ready to obey.

"Horus will have you at the palace now."

Kai looked around to see where exactly it was that she had been taken. She could see the mighty river that had been turned to blood. The Nile. And she could see the field where she had first met Amenken.

Where are you, friend?

The three huge men walked Kai to the pharaoh's palace and took her to a small room just inside one of the building's many entrances. Everywhere she looked, gnats littered the ground. One of the guards broke away and went into a closet of sorts and came back out with a tool that looked like a shovel.

"You will use this to start cleaning up the mess that you brought with you."

Kai took the shovel and started scooping up a pile of gnats.

"Horus is on his way to give you more instructions." The guards left the same way they came in.

Kai thought about running again, but she knew she wouldn't get far. She took the shovel loaded with gnats and dumped it back outside on the ground near the walking path. She went back inside and repeated the shoveling and dumping process several times, until the room she was standing in was cleared of the gnats.

As she turned to go and start cleaning out the next room, Kai saw Horus. He was walking with a very battered version of Amenken. Her friend was bleeding on his arms and chest.

"Ah, Kai. I'm glad to see you didn't try to run. Cooperating is always your best option."

"Amenken!"

Horus spoke before Amenken had a chance to. "Kai, the more information you keep from me, the worse your friend here is going to feel."

"I told you I don't know anything!"

The falcon stepped closer so he was just inches from Kai's face.

"I believe you believe that. But there is some connection between this traitor here"—Horus pointed to Amenken—"and the Israelite girl. And somehow, you and those two know something about these plagues. Tell me and all the hurting will end."

"I have told you the truth." Kai took a deep breath and repeated a quick silent prayer for God to give her strength to boldly stand up to this man. "But what I haven't told you is that these plagues won't stop until people lose their lives."

"See, I knew you had information about why these plagues are happening to us. Keep talking and your friend will be spared further pain and suffering."

Kai wanted to help Amenken. The only information she had was what she read in the Bible. She told the falcon that there would be a total of ten plagues, and then Moses would successfully lead the Israelites out of captivity. That Pharaoh would send his soldiers after them, but the Red Sea would part and God would make a way for all the people to find freedom.

Horus just stood there looking at her like she was next in line to take the lunatic title away from old man Naaji.

"Okay, Kai. Let's just say this bizarre story of yours was true. I'm going to keep you around in case there is another plague. I will keep you with me so that whatever is protecting you will also cover me."

Kai wanted all of this to end. She was ready to go home and forget that the trip to Egypt and the plagues ever happened. "I'm not going to help you. I know how this ends. God's in control, not you."

Horus laughed. His world was moved by the powerful. Pharaoh spoke and people went into action. No one questioned his authority because those who did met with serious consequences. "Kai, even though I believe none of what you're saying, you have something about you that is quite powerful. The plagues stay away from you."

"God is in control. For some reason, I'm not being bothered by them, just like the Israelites in the valley are not being bothered by them." Kai felt stronger now as she spoke truth to this Egyptian bully.

"I don't have time to listen to your make-believe stories. I'm going to have my men take you right next to the palace, where you will spend every one of your daylight hours cleaning up the fields."

Horus said something to one of his guards that Kai couldn't understand. The same guard grabbed Kai by the hand and led her down the palace steps, out across the wide street, and into the fields that were covered with remnants of frogs and gnats.

As the soldier stood next to Kai, a second guard came up behind them holding a rake. He didn't get a chance to give Kai instructions because a loud buzzing sound pulsed through the air around them. The guards instinctively looked back to the palace.

Dark swarms of tiny bugs flew into the pharaoh's home. The guards looked at Kai then back at each other. They didn't know what to do with her.

The buzzing got louder, and the swarms multiplied.

Flies.

They swarmed over the guards but left Kai alone. The guards tried using their hands to swat the flies away from their faces. No use.

The noise became so loud that Kai couldn't hear the guards even though they were no more than six feet away from her.

Flies were appearing out of thin air and were literally turning the day to night.

The guards picked up Kai and carried her back in the direction of the palace. The flies continued to swarm around the guards' faces, so thick that they couldn't make it ten feet without stopping to recalculate their direction. Keeping Kai close to them didn't change the situation.

They put her down and used their hands to swat at the flies.

Then came a wicked swirl of commotion as even more flies swarmed them. There were so many flies, it looked to Kai like the guards were getting swallowed up by an ocean of black water. She heard the guards but could no longer see them. Everything she saw was flies. But for some crazy reason, the flies were not bothering her. It was like she was standing in the eye of a dark hurricane.

A second unexplainable event came quickly. A woman appeared, stepping right out of a wall of flies.

It was Amenken's wife.

"Betrest!"

The woman stood before Kai, holding out something in her hands.

The flies stayed back, leaving the older woman alone too.

"Kai, I am sorry for the way I treated you," Betrest said as she stared at the ground. "I was scared and didn't know what was going on. My husband calmed my nerves as he explained your real character and how you wanted to protect that Israelite girl."

Kai was grateful the woman spoke those words. "I've been scared too, but the longer I'm in your world, the more confidence I find to believe in myself."

Betrest finally looked up at Kai. "Amenken told me to give this to you."

Now that Kai was closer, she could see that Betrest held a small silver blade.

"My husband made this weapon for himself. To keep us safe. Once Horus started coming around asking questions about you and Lily, Amenken told me about this blade."

Kai took the blade and turned it over in her hands. It was surprisingly heavy for its small size. That's when she saw the red gemstone above the handle. This was the same blade that Amenken had shown her the first time she was in his house. The same blade that meant so much to him.

"It was his prized possession. The highlight of his talents." Betrest spoke with words that were wrapped in sadness given the irony of the situation. The blade that her husband had made to protect them could not keep the beatings from happening. Horus had found a way to inflict pain on Amenken, and this beautiful dagger did nothing to prevent it.

"Thank you, Betrest." Kai had never held anything like this weapon before.

"My husband said that you will be the one to defeat Horus. And between you and me, I believe him. There is something special about you that speaks of courage and bravery."

Kai had nothing more to say. Here in this other-world, she was becoming a strong person who wasn't being ruled by fear. "Thank you."

"Horus captured Lily to use for bait to lure you and my husband in. I saw them take her into the building we call the Halls. It's the building next to the palace on the northeast side. You will see a large statue of a man. The Halls is right past the statue. Right over there." Betrest pointed and Kai looked in the right direction. Because of the flies nothing was clear, but she thought she could make out the outline of a statue.

"Thank you," Kai said as she hugged Amenken's wife.

"Go, young one, and teach that bully a lesson."

Kai smiled and, dagger in hand, took off running toward the Halls.

CHAPTER 7

Even though the flies didn't plague her, Kai found it difficult to run through the swarms on her way.

The sun was beginning to set, and Kai wondered how long it would take to get Lily out. Kai might have to wait, and she mentally geared herself up for a night of rough sleep on a hard floor inside the Halls building. Running with the dagger made her feel stronger with each step. There was a bigger reason for her being here, and sleeping comfortably had nothing to do with it.

Kai hurried on through the dusty village streets, still amazed that the flies somehow left her alone. The tiny creatures were buzzing and swarming around and over everything in sight. The villagers were shouting and screaming their complaints about this insane insect invasion.

Kai kept her eyes peeled for any soldiers eager to bring her back to Horus. So far, so good. Everyone she passed was preoccupied with trying to rid themselves of the flies.

As she came up to the towering statue, Kai looked around and found the building she needed. She didn't want to go running into the main entrance and not give herself a chance of reaching Lily. Betrest didn't mention any other entrances, so Kai started on the right side and began to look for one. She walked all the way around the building without finding an alternative way in. There was only the main entrance.

Lord, be with me!

Kai lifted the dagger in front of her and entered slowly through the huge doorway. She kept expecting soldiers to jump out at her, but they didn't. No one approached her as she slipped further into the darkness of the temple. It would have been helpful to know exactly where inside the building Lily was being kept.

The swarming flies were so numerous and their

movements so erratic, they extinguished all the wall torches inside the temple, leaving Kai to wade through the dim interior.

Kai decided to go right, making sure she kept her back to the outside wall and the dagger pointed out in front. One of the first things she noticed was that this building also had pillars like the temple. But here they weren't as tall.

A noise stopped her in her tracks. Kai could make out voices. They were coming from inside the Halls. Men. And they were close by. Kai couldn't understand what they were saying, but it didn't sound like they were wishing each other a good day. Kai crept closer. In the faint light that remained, she could make out two men, one who was dressed like Horus and the other like the guard who had walked her to the fields. Just past the men was a smaller alcove and a door.

Kai guessed that Lily had to be close by.

After another round of loud talking, the man dressed like Horus left and walked out of the building.

Kai propped her body against one of the stone pillars so she had a clear view of the entrance door and also the alcove where she felt certain Lily was being held. If the lone guard left his post, Kai would be ready to move. She didn't want to risk falling asleep and then being found, but sleep was coming for her and she couldn't resist.

ooooo

When she opened her eyes, it took a second to remember where she was. Kai had lost track of time but guessed she had been asleep for a while. The guard was still at his post even though the flies were still swarming around him.

As she sat and stared at the guard, an unexpected thing happened. In the time it took Kai to blink, the flies dropped to the ground. Not one left to buzz around. All of them fell to the floor like one big black tarp had dropped from the ceiling.

At first she thought she was dreaming, but she tapped the end of the dagger and felt its sharp point pinch her skin. She was awake, and when she blinked a second time, all of the flies that had blanketed the ground disappeared.

Terrified, the guard took off running toward the entrance.

This was her chance. Kai sprinted across the middle of the building and reached the alcove unseen. She looked back and didn't see the guard. She saw the door and pushed on it, but it wouldn't budge. There was no knob on it like the doors back home. She knew the guard could be back any second. Kai knocked and waited. She looked back and still no guard.

Come on.

Kai wanted to call Lily's name but didn't want the guard to hear if he was close by.

The door swung open. Lily stood there looking at Kai. "Lily!"

The little girl smiled and jumped into Kai's arms. Kai held her in a big bear hug then looked over the girl's shoulder and counted eleven other children.

"We have to hurry. Is there another way out?" Kai wanted to ask what on earth Pharaoh needed with twelve kids but knew that it wasn't the right time.

"Yes," Lily said. "Back there, but they have a guard there too."

Kai was ready to take a chance. She knew that the guard on this side was coming back because he had left his post. Maybe there wasn't a guard on the other side. And if there was, maybe the massive fly death moved him to run and tell somebody too. She'd go out first and find out.

She had Lily and the other kids hurry over to the back door. Then Kai closed the near door. Hopefully when the guard came back, he wouldn't have a desire to check on the twelve prisoners.

The room was small and took only ten strides to cross. Kai quickly found the door. She took a deep breath and gripped the dagger. She opted for the element of surprise and kicked the door open.

No one there. She was looking at an empty hallway. Quickly, she ushered the children out of the room and then shut the door behind her.

Kai led them carefully in the direction of the main entrance, keeping the dagger ready and her eyes peeled for any signs of the enemy.

"Are you Kai?"

Kai froze. She couldn't see the owner of the deep voice. She had been so careful, only to be caught by a phantom.

"Kai, is that you?"

She didn't answer. The children had stopped too, waiting for their rescuer.

"Kai, Betrest sent me."

Kai squinted and saw the man standing by a far pillar off to her right. A guard would have snuck up and captured her without warning. She had to decide quickly....

"Yes, can you get us out?"

"Follow me."

Kai motioned for the children to follow her as she walked through the dark shadows in the path that the man took. After a few twists and turns down narrow stone hallways, the whole group stepped out into the Egyptian city. There were no signs of guards or anyone else.

The sun was starting to rise over the horizon, painting the sky in many shades of red and orange.

I must have been asleep a lot longer than I thought.

"There is a secret tunnel that cuts through the back side of the fields. I will show you where. You and the children will take that. It will drop you by the lake. Go left and you will eventually reach the camp."

Kai followed the man, making sure all the children were accounted for. Just as they were reaching the fields, Kai looked back and saw an Egyptian official on horseback galloping up the path. The man was wearing a primitive uniform that consisted of only a linen kilt around his waist and leather sandals on his feet.

"Hurry!" The man led them to the edge of the fields where large rectangular stones had been piled on top of each other. It reminded Kai of that Jenga game where you made a tower out of wooden blocks and tried to keep it from tipping over. "Back here."

Kai knew they weren't going to make it. The official had closed the distance between them. And then as if things couldn't get any more bizarre, Kai stared in disbelief as the horse collapsed in midstride, sending the rider flying.

"Come on!"

Kai ran behind the boulders and saw a large opening in the ground. She followed the last child down steps that disappeared into the cold, wet earth.

CHAPTER 8

When Kai stepped out of the other end of the earthen tunnel, she noticed the ground went down a hillside and ended at the bank of a waterway.

Lily was standing off by herself. There were two donkeys lying next to each other on the ground by her feet.

Kai had no idea what to say to Lily. This had to be the next plague where all the land's livestock were affected. First the horses back by the palace had been struck down, and now the donkeys.

"I'm sorry. I'm sure they didn't feel a thing."

Kai tried guiding the young girl away from the fallen animals. "We need to hurry, Lily."

They all started running toward the valley where Lily and the other Israelite children lived. That's when Kai saw a group of Egyptian soldiers guarding the path that led to the tent city. Two of the soldiers began running up the hill toward the girls.

"Come on," Kai said. "Let's head down toward the river."

All along the hillside, cows and sheep were lying, on their sides, dead.

God, help us!

Kai and the other children navigated a course through the animals and made it to the water.

The river was wide but not deep. Kai went first to make sure the others could cross. The soldiers were half-way down the hill.

Kai waded back through the rushing water to help get all the children to the other side.

The soldiers were closing in fast.

A wind came out of nowhere, making it hard to see as water blew around in swirls of whitecaps and sprays of mist.

Tiny black flakes floated over the hillside, pouring down from the direction of the palace. It looked like a rain of dark dust falling on the kids, the animals, and the soldiers. As soon as the soldiers reached the water, they stopped.

Kai looked back and cringed. As the black flakes touched the soldiers' skin, their skin turned to splotchy red bumps. The grown men cried out in pain. Catching the kids was now the least of their worries.

Even though the same dark dust flakes rained over Kai and the children, they weren't bothered by it.

"Come on!"

Kai led the children toward the valley, hoping the soldiers wouldn't follow.

ooooo

Thunder rocked the world and everything in it.

Kai and the children kept running.

Lightning flashed.

Toward the valley. . .

Cold air ripped across the plain pushing trees back and forth.

The single soldier still behind them, making his way closer. . .

Wind gusts began to rage, a sure sign that something much fiercer was on its way.

The falcon. . .

Water fell in heavy drops splattering across the earth.

The drops turned to ice.

The land was beaten under the icy force.

Every tree was stripped bare.

The seventh plague.

ooooo

Kai and the children ran on.

Winged insects followed the chilly tempest, devouring everything left in the fields. Nothing green remained.

Toward the valley. . .

Strong winds came from the east, blowing locusts in all day and all night until the earth was black. The insects devoured all the fruit that hung from battered tree branches.

It was hard to run against the force of the wind, but Kai and the children didn't quit. The locusts didn't bother them.

Please, God, help us!

A west wind came and blew the locusts into the Red Sea—a watery grave for the eighth plague.

Kai and the children ran on. . .

. . .toward the valley.

ooooo

The Egyptian sky looked like it was being controlled by a dimmer switch, as if some invisible hand was sliding it down to make the heavens go dim.

Kai and the children moved quickly through the empty trees that had been torn apart by the hail. Experiencing these plagues made the Vivian Gold event a big joke. It was nothing compared to what Kai was going through here in this ancient place.

The darkness grew stronger, falling like blankets from the sky to smother those bound by gravity.

Would Kai ever see her family again? Was she ever going to leave this place? The barren landscape reflected her weary spirit. This other place—other time—had finally depleted her hope.

In a great moment of despair, Kai saw a pinprick of light in the distance—out over the valley. A beautiful light in the darkness.

Kai and Lily held hands as they continued on with the others.

It became harder and harder to see.

No moon or stars guided their way.

A sound of footsteps came from behind. The loose outline of a person stood out from the shadows.

The uniform. The soldier had finally caught up to them.

Kai told Lily to keep running with the other children.

"Don't stop until you make it to the camp."

Lily gave Kai a thumbs-up sign.

"Go!"

On her left, the children took off into the darkness. On her right, a nameless soldier came closer, ready to take care of Kai once and for all. Kai couldn't tell if there was just one soldier or many. It didn't matter.

As long as the children made it back to the valley.

CHAPTER 9

The brilliant sunrise brought with it more than just a new day. It brought signs of change and horrible things never before seen.

But it wasn't the sunlight that woke Kai from her light sleep; it was a distant sound of crying. At least she thought so. It seemed like the wind was wailing, expressing some supernatural sadness that couldn't be understood.

She rubbed her eyes and thought about all the plagues from the Bible account. If the last one she felt was darkness, then...

The guard who had been in charge of Kai came up and unlocked her cell. He motioned for her to step out. He had Amenken's dagger in his left hand.

Kai stayed in the cell.

"I've been charged with taking you with me. Horus wants you to draw Lily out, and then I will be there to take her."

Kai couldn't do it. As easy as it was to go along with the guard and save her own life, Kai could not trick Lily like that. "I can't."

The guard smiled. "That's the lack of food talking. It will be okay. The pharaoh has a great meal prepared if you help us get Lily back."

"What's with the dagger?" Kai knew the answer but wanted to make sure.

"If you decide not to help"—the guard raised the dagger. "You understand."

She did understand. But, no matter what, Kai wasn't going to bring any harm to Lily by her selfish decisions. "I do understand. And I can't help you."

The man reached out and grabbed Kai's arm. He yanked her out of the cell.

"One last chance. Will you help us or not?" His grip tightened. Any tighter and Kai thought her arm might break.

"I will not help you because—"

The guard's grip loosened.

Kai never had to finish her sentence. She looked up into the soldier's eyes. Just a second ago his eyes were filled with the pleasure of capturing her, but now they appeared lost and scared. They looked past Kai to some unseen point on the horizon.

And then, in the time it took Kai to blink, the guard collapsed on the ground in front of her. For a second, Kai stood there not understanding what happened. And then she remembered that the last plague attacked the ones who were born first in their families.

Kai bent down and picked up the dagger that had fallen to the ground along with the guard. She turned around and took off running toward the valley. She needed to catch up with Lily and her family. If the last plague had indeed come over the land, then the Israelites would be leaving for good. Kai had to hurry and join them before it was too late.

ooooo

Kai arrived in the valley and found it eerily empty. The tents were vacant, like an army of ghosts waiting patiently to be put to use. She ran up and down the paths that divided the tent city and didn't see any signs of life.

This was the end. Moses had led the Israelites away from here. The exodus had begun.

Kai had been obsessed with saving Lily and never gave thought to what she would do now. Somewhere in the middle of the sea of tents she stopped to pray.

God, how do I get out of here?

Where do I go?

Help me!

The only option that made sense was to catch up with the Israelites and be with Lily. They couldn't have gone too far.

Kai took off running again, this time in the direction of the east end of the valley. Away from Egypt. Away from the pharaoh. Away from Horus.

It was the only plan she had. Her only choice. Run to the east and join the others. Start a new life with Lily and her family, and keep hoping that one day she would be reunited with her own family back in Florida.

The empty rows that once contained an endless array of tents flashed by on either side of her. Kai could see the edge of the settlement, where the valley started and spread out in a wide-open plain. And she also saw *people*! A sea of Israelites. There they were. . .no more than a mile away!

Kai kept running, picking up speed like a train going down the tracks. Only a few more rows and then the open valley.

Until her plan came to a wicked end, as a horse and rider appeared from behind the last row of tents, blocking her way to the valley beyond.

Horus.

CHAPTER 10

The falcon dismounted and walked over to Kai. He was holding Naaji's journal in his left hand.

"I have to give you credit. You'd make a fine soldier. You have integrity."

God, please protect me!

Kai versus the falcon. There was no way out, except through the bully.

"If God is for me. . ." Kai lifted the dagger.

Horus inched closer, keeping his eye on the blade.

"You should have accepted the offer to help us." He held up the journal. "I don't know what this is about, but after I finish you, it won't matter."

The falcon inched closer. Closer to its prey.

Kai backed away from the official.

"You are about to feel the consequence of your bad decision."

Horus jumped at her, moving fast like a bolt of lightning.

Kai tried using the dagger to defend herself, but the grown man was too fast and too strong.

The falcon pinned her to the ground. There was no way out.

The dagger had slipped out of Kai's hand and landed on the ground, just beyond her reach.

Kai had failed. She was finished.

She thought of Lily. This whole experience couldn't end like this.

Just then Kai had a random memory. Language Arts. Mr. Kay read the book *Poppy* to the class. Kai loved it because the little deer mouse, Poppy, figured out a way to outwit and stand up to the evil great horned owl, Mr. Ocax. In the end, justice was served. Just the same way she saw Moses deal with the pharaoh. He wasn't afraid to stick up for God. Moses believed that he was sticking up for God's people by standing up to the Egyptian leader.

If Moses could stand up to Pharaoh, I can stand up to this guy.

As the falcon leaned closer, Kai spit in his face.

He shut his eyes, and Kai rolled over and grabbed the dagger. She jumped to her feet and in the same motion spun around and kicked the soldier in the knee like she was a professional soccer player blasting a ball for the game-winning goal.

The soldier hunched over and dropped the journal.

Kai didn't waste any time.

She grabbed the book and ran to the horse.

Horus stood up and somehow managed to run after her.

"You can't beat me, Kai from Florida! I'm too strong for you."

Kai tried to jump up on the horse, but it was too tall.

Horus was almost on her again.

Kai managed to get one foot in the left stirrup and pull herself up to stand.

Horus moved to pull her off the horse, but Kai used her other hand to swing the dagger at him. She grabbed hold of the saddle and pulled herself up to a sitting position.

Kai used her legs to kick the horse into a gallop.

Come on!

But the horse didn't move.

Horus stood there considering her. "It's over, Kai. Just get down and I'll—" He lunged and grabbed on to her left leg. She plunged the dagger into the falcon's hand.

He didn't scream. Horus simply removed the dagger just as simply as if he had removed a watch from his wrist.

The horse began to run, knocking Kai off balance, but she managed to hold on.

She had escaped the evil one.

Thank You, God.

CHAPTER 11

The horse galloped hard beneath her. Powerful muscles exploded, moving the animal and rider rocket-like, away from the predator.

Kai felt as though she were flying across the Egyptian landscape. Her whole body was filled with renewed energy and excitement as the horse carried her toward freedom. After everything she had gone through saving Lily from Horus, racing away and knowing that now she would be saved was a perfect ending to a most epic adventure.

A hundred yards away, two massive walls of water had been pulled back to expose a narrow stretch of dry land. The Red Sea. The freedom path. She could see the last of the Israelites safely reaching the far shore.

Just like the Bible said they did!

Kai kicked her legs, trying to spur the horse on. All she had to do was reach the other side of the water before the walls collapsed.

Behind her, a second horse, mounted by an Egyptian guard, closed the gap. The chase was finally over.

How did he catch up so fast?

Even though Kai had put up an honorable fight, the pharaoh's warrior was seconds away from catching his human prey. He rode up beside her and grabbed the back of her tunic. Kai tried pushing his arm away, but her horse was moving too fast and the falcon was too strong.

Only a short time before, she had been standing at the edge of the Pi-Hahiroth camp, overlooking the sea.

Her heroic fight and escape meant nothing.

Horus squeezed hard and yanked her body from the fleeing horse.

The guard threw her body down, into the water.

It felt like she had hit dry ground.

Ahead, on the freedom path, Kai focused on the thousands of men and women who were marching on, celebrating their epic escape from captivity. Lily was there. At least something good came from the ordeal.

The force of hitting the water stunned Kai. She lost her bearings. Her body turned numb. The warrior had dismounted and was standing over her. Pure evil poured from his eyes.

The end was here. The only thing Kai could think about was the little girl. At least she was free. Never to be bullied by the wicked man standing over her. Then Kai realized she was still holding on to Naaji's journal!

The soldier who had been pursuing her since Goshen reached down and yanked Kai to her feet. The man's free hand moved to slap Kai's face. She managed to reach out and block the shot with one hand. Anger tightened the man's grip.

Ahead, the sea of people continued on, moving toward a new reality. A reality that included freedom and experiencing the satisfaction that came from making their own choices. In all their celebrating, Kai's call for help was drowned out. She was past the point of being saved.

"You were a fool to think you'd escape!"

The words that came from the soldier's mouth were truth now.

They took on form and entered Kai's mind like Amenken's dagger. Kai felt them penetrate her spirit and release the last drops of willpower she'd been holding on to.

The earth made a weird groaning, and then it grew louder and sounded like cars crashing. Metal being twisted and pulled apart and twisted again. It made Kai think of an aluminum can being crushed under the force of a sledgehammer.

Water started shooting off both sides of the walls, back and forth over the path.

She took one last look at the Israelites and saw them vanish as the massive walls of water slammed shut over the narrow path of dry ground.

The sea quickly wrapped Kai up in its waves and carried her away. She saw Horus and the other guard being sucked into the sea's darkness.

The fight was over.

And so was Kai.

CHAPTER 12

PRESENT DAY

"Open her eyes!"

She could hear the rain splattering hard across the pavement. The water made a ringing sound, and Kai pictured a huge giant dropping an endless supply of nails all over the ground.

"Come on, Kai."

Kai opened her eyes and saw a blue shirt soaked in water. Her brain quickly pieced it all together. She wasn't in Egypt but back home in Florida! She remembered Vivian shoving her, and arms catching her as she fell. Arms covered in a blue dress shirt.

Kai looked up and saw Vivian Gold standing over her. Just like the falcon. Rain pouring over them just like the Red Sea crashing down around her and Horus.

Kai stared at Vivian.

Kai looked back over her shoulder and saw that the person wearing the blue shirt wasn't a teacher like Kai had originally thought.

"I don't have time to watch you sit here and cry like a baby," said Vivian.

No more, thought Kai.

She rolled to her right and jumped up. "Get away from me!"

Vivian brushed her hands over her wet shirt and laughed. "Really? You wanna go there?"

Now Kai remembered hearing a teacher's voice as she lay on the sidewalk. She looked around but didn't see any adult from school. The crowd of kids had disappeared.

It was just Kai and Vivian and the rain. And the man wearing the blue dress shirt.

"Need help?"

"She doesn't need any help," said Vivian. "Do you, Kai?"

"Who are you?"

"I'm Mark Grant."

Mark Grant?

"Who?"

"Mark Grant. You dropped your book." The stranger handed her the journal she had taken from Horus. *Old man Naaji's journal.*

Kai recalled looking at the old man's sketchbook. Her mind flashed the name *MARK GRANT*.

No way! Kai couldn't believe what she was seeing.

Vivian was ready to finish Kai. "Let's go, Kai. I'm done."

Kai felt a surge of energy fill her body. She took the journal.

Kai was ready to face her fears. The whole interaction with the Egyptian escape filled her heart with courage. . . .

Even if she had imagined the whole thing, Kai felt an energy flowing through her that hadn't been there before.

"Kai, do you need help?"

She looked at the newcomer. She nodded.

Mark Grant turned to Vivian. "I think we're done here."

The man stepped in between Kai and Vivian.

"Really, Kai? You want some stranger to save you?

Too bad you don't want to hang out with me. We could make a good team."

"Why don't you leave? I'm going home now," Kai said.

Vivian laughed. "You're a joke, Kai. You walk around the whole school and neighborhood like you're some queen who's better than everybody else. I'm sick of it!"

Vivian moved in and shot her hands out to shove Kai, but Mark Grant stepped to the side and used both of his hands to hold Vivian back.

Kai didn't back down. "You're done, Vivian. I don't want to fight you, but you are not going to bully me anymore."

Vivian just laughed again. "You're lucky this dude is here to keep me from hurting you."

"Vivian, I just fought a grown man. You've got nothing compared to what I experienced."

The bigger girl looked at Kai and shook her head. "You are whacked out of your mind. I'm telling my mother that you hit me. She'll call the school, and you'll be suspended."

"You'd better leave me and the other kids alone,

Vivian. I'm sick of your bullying."

Vivian clenched her fist and made a move like she was going to punch Kai. But this time Kai didn't flinch. She just stood there, strong and brave. Unmoving.

Vivian threw a real punch this time, aimed directly at Kai's chest. But now Kai was quicker. She moved her right arm in a counterclockwise motion and successfully blocked Vivian's arm, knocking the bully off balance.

"You're weird, Kai. *Weird.* I'm done wasting my time with you. I'll get you next time when your bodyguard here isn't around."

Kai didn't speak. She stood her ground and watched as Vivian turned and walked away.

When Kai was confident that Vivian Gold wasn't coming back, she started walking home. She wanted to talk to Mark Grant but felt it was best to go so her parents wouldn't worry. She stopped and turned back. "Thank you for helping me."

The man smiled. "Not a problem. If you ever need anything, my family and I live just down the street. 33 Jacaranda Court. You and your parents are always invited."

Then Kai remembered the book she was holding. "What is this?"

Mark Grant shrugged his shoulders. "I saw it on the ground and assumed it was yours."

Kai flipped through the journal pages until she got to the page that had Mark's name and picture. "Look. We're both in here." She held out the journal for the man to see.

"That's me, all right. Kai, uh, this is going to sound crazy, but I've had a handful of experiences like the one you just had."

Kai looked at the man and considered his words. She didn't know what to say. How did this guy know what she just went through?

Mark Grant continued talking. "I've been to the ark and met Noah and his sons. I went through Egypt and witnessed the plagues—"

"Wait! Egypt?"

"Yes, Egypt. I saw the plagues, and I also met the old man who made that journal you're holding."

Her brain was overloaded from all the things she had just seen in Egypt. *Hashtag mind blown.* Now, she was trying to process the fact that this man standing in front of her claimed to have witnessed the same. Nothing in her short life could have prepared her for the experience and nothing could ever take it away. She believed that things always happened for a reason, but Kai had no idea what the point of the whole thing was.

"This is crazy."

Mark Grant kept smiling. "I know. But, the fact that you have the journal means that things are changing."

Kai thought for a second. "The old man said something about I have to decide what to do with the journal."

"Your story doesn't end here in Egypt."

"I think you will have more journeys. I think the people in that book are seeing events like you just saw for a reason. I believe that an epic battle of good and evil is coming. . .one much greater than you and I versus all the Vivian Golds of the world. I think there will be a way that you and I and everyone else in that journal will have to join together and do something big to help people see truth."

Kai heard the man's words but was too distracted by all the things she had just experienced.

"Don't worry, Kai. Just hold on to the journal."

A young girl joined them on the sidewalk. Kai hadn't noticed her before. She looked like Lily!

"Thank you," the girl said.

Kai looked at Mark Grant and then down to the girl. "For what?"

The little one playfully bounced in place. "For helping me."

"How have I helped? I don't even know you."

"That mean girl, Vivian."

Kai nodded. "Yeah, what about her?"

"Well, she has a friend who has been bothering me. I watched how you just stood up to her and it was awesome. That's what I'm gonna do too!"

"I'm Kai. What's your name?"

"Lily."

No way! "Hi, Lily! I'm glad I could help. You know, I just learned a big lesson."

Lily stopped bouncing. "What lesson?"

"Well, we may have a lifetime of bullies, but we have to remember that God is always with us and He never leaves our side. He'll protect us and help us stand up to them."

"Okay. Sounds good." And just as quickly as she had appeared, the little girl took off and was gone.

Kai smiled. She made a mental note to keep her eye out for the girl at school. If she could, Kai would make sure Vivian's pals left her alone.

Mark Grant put his hands together like he was praying. "You better get home now so your parents don't worry."

"Okay. Thanks again for helping me."

"Not a problem. Just hang on to the journal, and when the time is right, you and your parents are welcome to come to my house. You can meet my family and we can figure things out."

Kai was exhausted. She thanked the man one last time then ran home, clutching the journal tightly as she went.

ooooo

"Amen."

Kai lifted her head and opened her eyes. Her dad just finished praying for their dinner. And after every prayer, he said *amen*. And after every *amen*, Kai thought of Amenken.

Like most meals she'd had during the last couple of months, Kai spent the time distracted. She'd eat a little bit and think a lot about all the things she saw on that crazy trip.

Egypt.

Moses.

The plagues.

The exodus.

The falcon.

Mark Grant.

She had a hard time sitting still. "Dad, may I be excused?"

"Sure, honey. Everything okay?"

"Yeah. I just want to take a walk."

"Sounds good. Want company?"

"Yeah." Kai liked it when her father walked down to the school playground with her.

When they reached the end of their street, her dad pointed at a crow that was sitting on the sidewalk. Kai noticed that the bird was in the exact same spot she had been when Vivian pushed her down.

The falcon.

Horus.

Months had passed since she imagined the ten plagues; and like snow in winter, the flashbacks kept coming. Coming more often with the passing of time. She thought that the whole thing would pass like a dream, but that wasn't the case.

Kai wanted to find Mark Grant and talk to him, but when she googled his address, she found no matches in her area. The only 33 Jacaranda Court that came up was in San Francisco, California. She tried riding her bike around the neighborhood looking for Mark Grant's street but came up empty. Where did the guy go? She remembered distinctly that he said he and his family lived right down the street. Odd.

As Kai and her father approached the crow, it looked as though it had been waiting on them, for as soon as they reached it, the bird took off. But it didn't fly away; it hovered in front of them as they walked to the school playground.

As they reached the swing set, the crow took off and flew away toward the school building. Kai followed its flight and watched as the bird headed toward the roof but then changed direction and flew over the back field. The crow touched down in a patch of tall grass just before the fence.

Kai thought she was flashing back to weirder days again because as the crow landed, a kaleidoscope of butterflies exploded up from the grass and filled the air.

"Dad, look!"

Kai jumped off the swing and made her way to the butterflies. They didn't fly away like the crow but stayed in a tight formation above the ground.

When Kai got close, the butterflies took off on a burst of wind.

She thought she must be losing her mind. Kai looked down and found a tree branch lying on the ground. It was a little longer than she was tall and slightly curved at one end.

Like a staff.

Just like Moses had!

She picked up the branch and turned it over in her hands, feeling its weight and surprisingly smooth edges.

Kai thought about dropping it and returning to the

swings. Then she remembered Moses using his staff to make all those crazy things happen back in Egypt.

"Is it okay if I bring this home?"

Her dad put his hands on her shoulders. "I don't get why you would want that branch, but I love you. If you want the branch, go for it!"

Kai knew why she wanted the branch. It made her feel strong. She tapped one end of the branch on the ground, but nothing happened. Did she expect another plague to rise up and cover her neighborhood? She grinned. *Oh well, it was worth a shot.*

They headed back to the playground. Kai asked her dad to hold the branch while she went down the slide. He looked like Moses standing there holding the staff. Minus the beard. It felt good to have fun. It felt good to be here, safe, with her father.

Yes, Kai would keep the branch. It was like a souvenir of her crazy journey back to Egypt. But not only was it a reminder of something that had happened in the past, the branch made her wonder about the future. Would there be another place she would *imagine*? Would there be another Bible story that would open up before her and bring her in? From the way Mark Grant talked, seeing more of the Bible stories wasn't out of the question.

Yes, Kai would keep the branch.

Just in case.

ABOUT THE AUTHOR

Matt Koceich is a husband, father, and public school-teacher. Matt and his family live in Texas.